Moby Dick
- Rehearsed

A Drama in Two Acts

by Orson Welles

Being an adaptation - for the
most part in blank verse - of
the novel by Herman Melville

A SAMUEL FRENCH ACTING EDITION

SAMUEL FRENCH

FOUNDED 1830

New York Hollywood London Toronto

SAMUELFRENCH.COM

ISBN   978-0-573-61242-8   Printed in U.S.A.   #700

MUSIC USE NOTE

IMPORTANT BILLING AND CREDIT REQUIREMENTS

MOBY-DICK—REHEARSED; presented at the Ethel Barrymore Theatre; an adaptation in two acts by Orson Welles of Herman Melville's novel, entire production staged by Douglas Campbell, lighting by Klaus Holm, incidental music by Harold Glick, presented by Jerry Adler and Samuel Liff with the following cast:

YOUNG ACTOR, later ISHMAEL ....*Bruno Gerussl*

AN ACTOR *with a newspaper* ....*Hugh Webster*

A MEMBER OF THE COMPANY ....*Bill Fletcher*

A MEMBER OF THE COMPANY, *later the* MASTHEADER *and the* VOICE OF THE BACHELOR ....*John Horton*

A SERIOUS ACTOR ....*Roy Poole*

A CYNICAL ACTOR ....*Max Helpmann*

A MEMBER OF THE COMPANY ....*Lex Monson*

A MEMBER OF THE COMPANY ....*Melvin Scott*

A MIDDLE-AGED ACTOR ....*Louis Zorich*

AN OLD "PRO" ....*David Thomas*

YOUNG ACTRESS ....*Frances Hyland*

STAGE MANAGER, VOICE OF THE RACHEL, *William Needles*

YOUNG ACTRESS'S UNDERSTUDY ....*Judith Doty*

THE ACTOR MANAGER ....*Rod Steiger*

Moby Dick—Rehearsed

ACT ONE

SCENE: *An American theatre at the end of the last century. Theatres are often cold during rehearsals, and the actors do not shed their long, dark overcoats except when the action, or the parts they are playing, would seem to demand shirt-sleeves. No stage properties are used. Harpoons, oars, lances, gold-pieces, prayer-books, charts and telescopes, all are to be indicated in gesture and mime. For easier reading only a minimum of stage directions are given in the text. The chase in the whale-boat, for example, is referred to briefly as literal action, with no attempt to describe the means by which the actors will suggest this in performance. It would not be true to say that there is no scenery. The stage is not bare; it is interestingly and even romantically dressed with all the lumber of an old-fashioned theatre.*

AT RISE: *An empty stage. Behind the usual forest of hanging ropes, suspended sandbags, battens, borders, furled back-drops and stacked wings, there is glimpsed the bare brick wall of the theatre. Here and there are the skeletons of stage platforms, on one of which stands a rather seedy-looking throne. At least two tables, a number of plain kitchen chairs and the sort of small upright organ called an harmonium. (This is actually an electric organ in disguise.) Beneath the shaded work-light a* YOUNG ACTOR *is studying a prompt-book. A* YOUNG ACTRESS *sits nearby, listening as he reads aloud:*

THE YOUNG ACTOR.
"Call me Ishmael. . . .

5

Some years ago—never mind how long—
I thought that I would sail about a little
and see the watery part of the world.
Whenever I grow grim about the mouth,
and hazy in eyes; whenever
it's a damp November in my soul;
I count it time to get to sea.
Almost all men, sometime or other,
cherish these same feelings toward the ocean. . . ."

(*Several* ACTORS *come on to the Stage during the following. They have arrived for a rehearsal.*)

". . . Here now is our island city
of a dreamy Sabbath afternoon;
what do you see? On every dock and wharf;
on the extremest limits of the land;
posted like sentinels: thousands of landsmen,
fixed in ocean reveries. . . ."

(*In partial silhouette, the mute figures of the* ACTORS *grouped near the edge of the Stage suggest an illustration of the spoken words.*)

"Inlanders of week-days tied to counters,
nailed to benches, clinched to desks.
Does the magnetic virtue of the compasses
of all those ships attract them thither?

Why did the old Persians hold the ocean
holy?—and the still deeper meaning
of that story of Narcissus, who, because
he could not grasp the mild, tormenting image
in the fountain, plunged into it, and drowned.
That same image we ourselves see in all rivers,
in oceans and in lakes and wells. The image
of the un-graspable—the phantom of life;
and this is the key to it all. . . ."

(*A short silence, then a burst of THUNDER! The* AC-
TORS *pay no attention to this, some lighting cigars*

or cigarettes, and one relaxing with a newspaper. The
THUNDER abruptly subsides and the STAGE MAN-
AGER, *in shirt-sleeves, pops his head out of the*
prompt-side of the proscenium arch.)

THE STAGE MANAGER. How's that?
THE YOUNG ACTOR. Fine. (*Turning to the* ACTRESS *as*
he closes the prompt-book.) That was a sort of prologue.
There are real scenes later on, of course—with dialogue.
A MIDDLE-AGED ACTOR. We know, laddie, we know.
God deliver us, we've been asked to learn enough of it!

(*Another sudden loud rumble of THUNDER, followed*
immediately by the reappearance of the STAGE MAN-
AGER.)

THE STAGE MANAGER. That was with the thunder sheet
instead of the drums.
THE YOUNG ACTOR. Fine.
A SERIOUS ACTOR. (*Speaking to one of the others.*) I
was wondering about my role— Oh, I beg your pardon,—
I don't think we've been introduced.
AN OLD "PRO." (*With cordiality.*) I know *you*, of
course;—Kent, Richmond, Iago, Mercutio, our new Sec-
ond Lead. (*Introducing himself.*) Eccentric Character,
First Comics and General Utility.

(*They shake hands.*)

THE SERIOUS ACTOR. How d'ye do.—Now, about this
"Starbuck" character I've been asked to memorize—
THE YOUNG ACTOR. (*Joining the group.*) That's the
First Mate, an honest, God-fearing sort of fellow. You
might say he's the only voice of sanity in the play.
A CYNICAL ACTOR. Sanity . . . ?

(*A sharp gust of WIND is heard; then sudden silence*
and the STAGE MANAGER *re-enters.*)

THE STAGE MANAGER. All right?

THE YOUNG ACTOR. Fine.

THE CYNICAL ACTOR. I didn't think there was anything about this whole project that wasn't every bit as certifiable—excuse me, laddie—as that one-legged old Captain in your book.

THE YOUNG ACTOR. Don't call it *my* book.

THE CYNICAL ACTOR. (*Rather huffily.*) Well, I can't call it anybody's *play;*—and the Governor is *your* Governor, laddie. You're the only one who could have talked him into this,—*whatever* it is.

THE YOUNG ACTRESS. As I understand it, this is to be a sort of reading—or rather a dress rehearsal without costumes or scenery.

THE YOUNG ACTOR. (*Briskly.*) That's right. Stop grousing, everybody; if it doesn't work we'll never do it again.

THE OLD "PRO." I'm thirsty. Isn't the Governor coming?

THE YOUNG ACTOR. Of course; he's doing Father Mapple's sermon and Ahab. We're all doubling parts, as you know. That's nothing new for this company. The stage manager's reading a few assorted voices in the ship's crew. You're Peleg—

THE OLD "PRO." (*Interrupting.*) Maybe, but I'm also thirsty.

THE YOUNG ACTOR. Don't worry, we'll take the curtain down after the second cabin scene—

THE STAGE MANAGER. Only one beer, gentleman, please —don't forget, we must be out of here in time to give the stagehands a chance to set up for tonight.

THE CYNICAL ACTOR. (*To the* YOUNG ACTOR.) Just as a point of information, laddie—have you led the Governor to believe that we can deliver him a shipwreck, a typhoon and a great white whale in this theatre—at a two-dollar top?

THE YOUNG ACTRESS. A white whale?

THE CYNICAL ACTOR. The title-role, my dear. One might have expected the Governor to be playing Moby

Dick himsef, but no, I understand he's to be invisible throughout. The whale, that is—not the Governor.

THE OLD "PRO." Of course it's invisible. My God, how could you put a thing like that on the stage?

THE ACTOR WITH THE NEWSPAPER. We could try. Uptown in Barnum's Museum there's a stuffed whale does more business on a Monday morning than we get in a week of Shakespeare—including matinees.

THE YOUNG ACTOR. (*Still speaking more to the* YOUNG ACTRESS *than to anyone else.*) The white whale is like the storm in "Lear"—it's real, but it's more than real;—it's an idea in the mind.

THE CYNICAL ACTOR. It's an idea in *your* mind, old boy.

THE YOUNG ACTRESS. "Lear's" what I was called to rehearse; but if you're doing this "Moby Dick" instead, there aren't any women's parts, so I guess I'm only needed for some music.

THE OLD "PRO." I remember when this company used to travel an orchestra.

THE ACTOR WITH THE NEWSPAPER. Yes, but the last few seasons the Governor's been economising with that harmonium.

(*The* GOVERNOR *enters during this last.*)

THE SERIOUS ACTOR. (*Who hasn't seen him.*) Harmonium—?

THE GOVERNOR. Why not?—Tum-tee-tum, Tum-tee-tum! On I come, and they love it. (*Murmurs of "Hello, Governor." The seated* ACTORS *rise. THE* GOVERNOR, *in his late sixties and with a noble mane of silver hair, is the classic actor-manager of the old school. His Inverness is high-buttoned and of such a sombre black as to be almost clerical. Until the "rehearsal" begins his face is shadowed by a broad-brimmed hat. He carries a stick which he now suddenly raises, pointing it at the* YOUNG ACTRESS.) "How now, Cordelia; mend your speech a little, Lest it may mar your fortunes." Three steps down right and bow. (*He makes the transition from Shakespeare to stage directions without a pause for breath.*)

THE YOUNG ACTRESS. "Good, my Lord,—"

THE GOVERNOR. Bow, dear—*bow;* don't duck. (*He sits in the throne.*)

THE YOUNG ACTOR. "You have begot me, bred me, lov'd me."

THE GOVERNOR. *Stand up* to me!

THE YOUNG ACTRESS. "I return those duties back as are right fit, Obey you—"

THE GOVERNOR. Last night you sounded like a parlour-maid who's broken a tea-cup—

THE YOUNG ACTRESS. (*A slight note of asperity creeping into the reading.*) "Obey you, love you, and most honor you— Why have my sisters, husbands,—"

THE GOVERNOR. Look to Goneril Left, speech, speech, look to Regan Right on "marry like my sisters to love my father all." "But goes thy heart with this?"

THE YOUNG ACTRESS. "Ay, good my Lord."

THE GOVERNOR. "So young and so untender?" Chin up, eyes flashing—

THE YOUNG ACTRESS. "So young, my Lord, and true."

THE GOVERNOR. (*Rising.*) "Let it be so, thy truth then be thy dower. Here I disclaim all my paternal care, Propinquity and property of blood—" Fall to your knees on blood, dear— "And as a stranger to my heart and me, Hold thee from this for ever. The barbarous Scythian"— You take that *down*stage, my dear—"Or he that makes his generation messes To gorge his appetite, shall to my bosom"— *Well down*stage, dear,—with your back to the audience; very bad for you, very good for me. Speech—speech "pitied and reliev'd As though my sometime daughter!"

THE SERIOUS ACTOR. (*As "Kent."*) "Good, my liege—"

THE GOVERNOR. (*Quietly business-like.*) Strike the throne.

THE SERIOUS ACTOR. (*Disappointed.*) Oh—we're not going on?

THE GOVERNOR. Today we're running through the new piece—

THE SERIOUS ACTOR. But regarding my role—

THE GOVERNOR. (*Cutting in.*) Your parts have all been assigned and, I trust, committed to memory. (*Turning back to the* YOUNG ACTRESS.) We'll try to squeeze in the "Tent" scene, my dear, sometime later. You really mustn't sob aloud, y'know, *all* through my "We two like birds i' the cage." It's distracting. (*Hands the* ASSISTANT STAGE MANAGER *a ring of keys.*) —Brandy.

(THE ASSISTANT STAGE MANAGER *departs. The throne is moved off and there is a preparatory bustle as* THE GOVERNOR *lights a cigar.*)

THE OLD "PRO." (*Under his breath.*) Pity . . .

THE ACTOR WITH THE NEWSPAPER. (*Folding the paper and putting it under his chair.*) What's a pity?

THE OLD "PRO." That we aren't going on with that; a real play, anyway—something you can *act.*

THE YOUNG ACTOR. (*Who has overheard this muttered exchange.*) Critics have even said that "Lear" can't be acted.

THE GOVERNOR. (*Who overheard* that.) Critics!

(*Several* VOICES *take up the war-cry.*)

THE STAGE MANAGER. Now, everybody! Let's not get started on the critics. There isn't time.—Places, please.

THE CYNICAL ACTOR. Well, at least "King Lear" was meant to be acted. This whale business was intended to be read.

THE YOUNG ACTOR. To be read aloud. There are things in it that simply have to be heard—

THE CYNICAL ACTOR. The Governor never should have allowed you to go to University, laddie—God deliver the Theatre from educated actors!

THE SERIOUS ACTOR. Because they're always trying to educate the public, you mean? Well—

(THE GOVERNOR *at his table has been occupying himself with the bottle of brandy* THE ASSISTANT STAGE MANAGER *has brought him, but at this last he turns on the other* ACTORS.)

THE GOVERNOR. Impertinence! We are the servants of the public! Just that;—servants. My God, gentlemen—how would you like to have to listen to uplifting lectures from your cook?

THE SERIOUS ACTOR. (*Rather intensely.*) Well, at least, sir,—you won't deny that the Theatre *needs poetry*—

THE GOVERNOR. (*Setting down the brandy bottle, with noisily impressive emphasis.*) When it *is* Theatre—the Theatre *is* poetry. True, when we do chestnuts like "The Bells" or "Spartacus," we aren't speaking poetry, but we are trying to make it. After all, that's our profession; one in which nothing is absolutely required except the actor:—and, of course, he only needs an audience.

THE CYNICAL ACTOR. (*Under his breath.*) Ask any unemployed actor—

THE YOUNG ACTOR. (*With a grin.*) And when the audience decides it doesn't need us—?

THE GOVERNOR. (*With massive deliberation.*) The audience—? Boy, they *never* need us! Nobody ever *needed* the Theatre, at all, except the people up on the stage. Did you ever hear of an unemployed audience? (*To the* STAGE MANAGER.) Shall we begin?

THE STAGE MANAGER. Places, please—

THE GOVERNOR. We'll be grateful for whatever help you can improvise for us with the lighting, Mr. Stage Manager, and for any sound effects you can manage. (*Shading his eyes from the glare of the footlights and peering out into the auditorium of the Theatre.*) Is the scenery fellow there?—Perhaps he'll get some notions from this run-through—

THE STAGE MANAGER. We used to do a pretty good ocean for the escape scene in "Monte Cristo," Governor.

THE GOVERNOR. I don't know—this is more like one of the Greek pieces. There are bound to be places where

we'll have to leave it to the words—and the imagination. (*Turning to the* CAST.) Gentlemen, your various roles have been assigned to you. Miss Jenkins, failing a small negro child we're going to ask you to read "Pip" the cabin-boy for us, just for today, and also to provide appropriate music— We'll run straight through no matter what happens—that is, unless we break down altogether, or our friends out there decide they've had enough. This time we're asking quite an extra bit of cooperation from them: They are to provide a ship, fully rigged, and a couple of oceans for us to sail it in. To crudely paraphrase a far more elegant apology than ours: (*He has turned frankly toward the audience by now and is speaking directly to them—*)
"Piece out our imperfections with your mind;
Think—when we speak of whale-boats, whales and oceans,
That you see them—For 'tis your thoughts
That now must deck our stage; jumping o'er time;
Turning the accomplishments of many years
Into an hour-glass . . ."

(*A moment's pause, the impressiveness of which is rather spoiled by:*)

THE SERIOUS ACTOR. Excuse me, just one word—
THE GOVERNOR. (*Not pleased.*) Well—?
THE SERIOUS ACTOR. About my role, this part of "Starbuck," I've been asked to get up in—
THE GOVERNOR. (*With elaborate patience.*) Well—?
THE SERIOUS ACTOR. I wondered just how you *see* it—the characterisation—?
THE GOVERNOR. (*Rather brusquely.*) First Mate of the whaling ship; stands up to the Captain—that's me—
THE SERIOUS ACTOR. (*Breaking in earnestly.*) Yes, I know, but what I *mean* is—since we're playing it together, what exactly do you want me to *do?*
THE GOVERNOR. *Do?* Stand six feet away and do your damndest!

(*He turns briskly Upstage. The WORK-LIGHT at the*

same moment switches out, and THE YOUNG ACTRESS
*plays a kind of "hurry music" by way of overture
on the harmonium. Led by* THE STAGE MANAGER,
*there is a flurry of efficient chair-moving and other
preparations; then—at his signal—the movement
freezes, and after a short silence—the play begins.
MUSIC: One of the* ACTORS *plays a mouth-organ in
the background.*)

THE STAGE MANAGER. (*Reading from his prompt-
book.*) "Scene: The wharf in Nantucket, the whaling ship
'Pequod' in the background. The owner Mister Peleg
discovered. Enter to him Ishmael.

ISHMAEL. Is this the Captain of the "Pequod"?

PELEG. S'posin' it be?

ISHMAEL. I was thinking of shipping.

PELEG. Ye were, were ye?—ever been in a stove boat?

ISHMAEL. No, sir, I never have.

PELEG. Know nothin' at all about whalin', I daresay
—eh?

ISHMAEL. I've no doubt I shall soon learn.

PELEG. Flukes! Man, what makes ye want to go
a'whalin'? Let me hear that afore I think of shippin' ye.

ISHMAEL. Well, sir. I want to see what whaling is.

PELEG. Are ye a man to pitch a harpoon down a live
whale's throat, and then jump in after it. Answer quick!

ISHMAEL. I am, sir, if it should be positively indispen-
sable to do so.

PELEG. Want to see what whalin' is, eh? Have ye
clapped eyes on Cap'n Ahab?

ISHMAEL. Who is Captain Ahab, sir?

PELEG. Captain of this ship.

ISHMAEL. I've mistaken me; I thought you were the
captain.

PELEG. Mister Peleg—that's who ye're speakin' to,
young man, I'm owner of the "Pequod." But if ye want
to know what whaling is I can put you in the way of
finding out. Clap eye on Cap'n Ahab, young man—and
ye'll find that Ahab only has one leg.

ISHMAEL. What do you mean, sir; was the other lost by a whale?

PELEG. Lost by a whale? Young man, come nearer to me: it was devoured, chewed up, crunched by the monstrousest, parmacetty that ever chipped a boat!—Still feel inclined for whaling?

ISHMAEL. I do, sir.

PELEG. Why?

ISHMAEL. I want to see the world, sir.

PELEG. Look out there—what d'ye see there?

ISHMAEL. Not much. Nothing but water; considerable horizon though, and a squall coming up.

PELEG. See the world, young feller? D'ye wish to go around Cape Horn to see any more of it? Can't ye see the world from where ye stand? (ISHMAEL *is at a loss for a reply.*) Think again, young feller—and once more again —afore ye bind yerself to anything past backin' out!

(*Exit* PELEG. *The mouth-organ has fallen silent.* ISHMAEL *remains Center Stage for the following soliloquy.*)

ISHMAEL.
What is it that so draws me now
to put down for a whaling voyage?—
The nameless undeliverable perils
of the great beast itself?—
The wild and distant seas wherein he rolls
his island bulk? I have an itch
for things remote . . . I'm quick to see a horror,
and be friendly with it, too;
for I prefer to be on friendly terms
with all the inmates of the place I lodge in. . . .

The flood-gates of the wonder-world
swing open; endless processions of the whale
float toward me; and above them all;
one grand and hooded phantom,
like a snow-hill in the air. . . .

(*MUSIC:* THE YOUNG ACTRESS *playing the harmonium; the other* ACTORS *singing.*)

ACTORS. (*Song.*)
> "The ribs and terrors of the whale,
> Arched over me a dismal gloom,
> While all God's sun-lit waves rolled by,
> And lift me deepening down to doom."

THE STAGE MANAGER. (*Reading from the prompt-book. The MUSIC continuing under his words.*)
"Scene—The Whaleman's Chapel in Nantucket.
Discovered: a small congregation.
Enter to them—Ishmael."

(*The* ACTORS *have removed their hats.* ISHMAEL *takes his place beside them. The HARMONIUM continues the melody of the hymn.*)

ISHMAEL. Few are the moody fishermen, shortly bound for the Indian Ocean or the Pacific, who fail to make a Sunday visit here. . . . The Chaplain has not yet arrived and silent islands of men and women steadfastly eye the tablets, black-bordered, masoned into the wall on each side of the pulpit.

(*THE* YOUNG ACTRESS *speaks up from her place at the harmonium, pronouncing "in character" the words of the first and last of the "tablets." A* CHORUS OF MEN, *from the midst of the congregation reads the legend on the second.*)

(VOICE OF WIDOW:)

SACRED
TO THE MEMORY
OF
THE LATE
CAPTAIN EZEKIEL HARDY
Who in the bows of his boat was
killed by a Sperm Whale on the
coast of Japan
August 3rd, 1833.

THIS TABLET
Is erected to his Memory
BY
HIS WIDOW.

. . . . . .

(CHORUS:)

SACRED
TO THE MEMORY
OF
ROBERT LONG, WILLIS ELLERY,
NATHAN COLEMAN, WALTER CANNY,
SETH MACY, AND SAMUEL GLEIG
Forming one of the boats' crews
of
THE SHIP ELIZA,
Who were towed out of sight by a
Whale, On the Off-shore Ground in the
PACIFIC
December 31st, 1839.
THIS MARBLE
Is here placed by their surviving
SHIPMATES.

. . . . . .

(WOMAN'S VOICE:)

SACRED
TO THE MEMORY
OF
JOHN TALBOT
Who, at the age of eighteen
was lost overboard, near the
Isle of Desolation, off Patagonia
November 1st, 1836.

THIS TABLET
Is erected to his Memory
BY HIS SISTER.

(The hymn again:)

ALL. *(Singing.)*
"In black distress, I called my God,
When I could scarce believe him mine,
He bowed his ear to my complaints—
No more the whale did he confine."
THE STAGE MANAGER. *(Reading.)* "Enter Father
Mapple. He ascends to the pulpit."

(THE GOVERNOR *has risen from his place by the prompt-
er's table. He faces directly forward towards the auditorium of the theater, his hands turning a page of
the prompt-book.*)

ALL. *(Singing.)*
"With speed he flew to my relief,
As on a radiant dolphin borne;
Awful, yet bright, as lightning shone
The face of my Deliverer God."

(*The hymn is finished. The* CONGREGATION *seat themselves, and after a pause, the* OLD MAN, *as* "FATHER
MAPPLE," *begins the sermon.*)

FATHER MAPPLE. Beloved shipmates, clinch the last
chapter of the first verse of Jonah—"And God has pre-
pared a great fish to swallow up Jonah."
Shipmates, the sin of Jonah was in his wilful disobedi-
ence of the command of God. He found it a hard command; and God's command *is* hard, shipmates—for in
obeying God, we must disobey ourselves. But Jonah still
further flouts at God by seeking to flee from him. Jonah
thinks that a ship, made by men, will carry him into
countries where God does not reign! With slouching hat
and guilty eye, prowling among the shipping like a vile

burglar hastening to cross the seas, at last, after much dodging search, he finds a ship receiving the last items of her cargo. As he steps aboard the sailors mark the stranger's evil eye. . . . "Point out my state-room," says Jonah. "I'm travel-weary; I need sleep." . . . "Ye looks it," says the Captain, "there's your room." . . . All dressed and dusty as he is, Jonah throws himself into his berth.

He finds the ceiling almost resting on his forehead; the air is close, and Jonah gasps. In that contracted hole he feels the heralding presentiment of that stifling hour when the whale shall hold him in the smallest of his bowels' wards.

And now the time of tide is come; the ship, careening, glides to sea. . . . But soon the sea rebels. It will not bear the wicked burden. A dreadful storm comes on; the ship is like to break, the bo'sun calls all hands to lighten her; boxes, bales and jars are clattering overboard; the wind is shrieking; the men are yelling. "I fear the Lord!" cries Jonah. "The God of Heaven who hath made the sea and the dry land!"—

Again the sailors mark him. The God-fugitive is now too plainly known. And wretched Jonah cries out to them to take him and cast him overboard,—for he knew that for *his* sake this dreadful tempest was upon them.

"And now behold Jonah taken up as an anchor and dropped into the sea"—into the yawning jaws awaiting him; and the whale shuts—to all his ivory teeth like so many white bolts upon his prison. Then Jonah prayed unto the Lord out of the fish's belly. But observe his prayer, shipmates. He doesn't weep and wail. He feels his punishment is just and leaves his deliverance to God.

Shipmates, sin not; but if ye do, take heed ye repent of it like Jonah.

And now—how gladly would I come down there and sit with you and listen while some one of *you* reads *me* the more awful lesson Jonah teaches me as a pilot of the living God. How, bidden by the Lord to preach unwelcome truths in the ears of the wicked, Jonah sought to escape his duty and his God by taking ship. But God is everywhere; and even "out of the belly of hell" God heard him when he cried. Then God spake unto the fish; and from the shuddering cold and blackness of the sea, the whale came breaching up to the sun, and "vomited out Jonah" upon the dry land; and Jonah—bruised and beaten—his ears, like two sea-shells, still multitudinously murmuring of the ocean—Jonah did the Almighty's bidding. And what was that, shipmates?—To preach the truth to the face of Falsehood!

Shipmates, woe to him who seeks to pour oil on the troubled waters when God has brewed 'em into a gale!— Who seeks to please rather than to appal! Yea, woe to him whose good name is more to him than goodness, and who—as the great Pilot Paul has it,—while preaching to others, is himself a castaway!

But oh, shipmates! Delight is to him—who, against the proud gods and commodores of this earth, stands forth, his own inexorable self!—who gives no quarter in the truth, and who destroys all sin though he pluck it out from under the robes of Senators and Judges! Delight— Top-gallant delight is to him who acknowledges no law or lord, but the Lord his God, and is only a patriot to Heaven. And eternal delight and deliciousness will be his, who, coming to lay him down can say—O Father!—mortal or immortal—here I die. I have striven to be Thine more than to be this world's, or mine own. Yet this is nothing; I leave eternity to Thee; for what is man that he should live out the lifetime of his God?

(*A silence. Then* THE STAGE MANAGER *speaks.*)

THE STAGE MANAGER. "Father Mapple remains at the pulpit until all the people have departed, and he is left alone in the chapel." (*A moment's silence. A change of LIGHTS.* ACTORS *re-enter at the back in shirt-sleeves to represent the crew of the "Pequod"; they busy themselves among the platforms and hanging lines—which are taken to be the ship. MUSIC: The mouth organ again.*

"FATHER MAPPLE" *has quietly left the Stage.* THE STAGE MANAGER *reads again from the prompt-book.*) "Scene— The whaling ship 'Pequod' upon the very point of starting for the voyage. Enter Ishmael, and afterwards to him Elijah, an old, mad sailor."

ISHMAEL. (*Looking at the ship, and cheerfully addressing the audience.*)
You may have seen many a queer craft
in your day, but take my word for it,
you've never seen a rare old craft
like this same rare old "Pequod"—
Weather-stained in the typhoons
of all the four oceans, her venerable bows
look bearded, and her three masts
stand like the spines of the three old kings
of Cologne. All worn and wrinkled
are her ancient decks; they made you think
of altar-stones in Canterbury
where Becket bled.

A noble craft, but somehow melancholy. . . .
All noble things are touched like that.
ELIJAH. (*Approaching* ISHMAEL.)
Have ye shipped in her?
ISHMAEL.
I've just now signed the articles. Good morning, sir.
ELIJAH.
Anything down there about your soul?
ISHMAEL.
                                   About *what?*

ELIJAH.
Mebbe ye haven't got any. No matter though.
Many young fellers haven't got any.
Good luck to 'em; they're all the better off for it.
A soul's a sort o' fifth wheel to a wagon.
He's got enough, though. *He's* got soul enough
to make up the deficiency of an entire crew.
Ye haven't *seen* Old Thunder, have ye?

ISHMAEL.
Old Thunder? And who's that?
ELIJAH.

Ahab. Cap'n Ahab.
Old Thunder is the name he goes by with some of us
old sailors. Ye haven't *seen* him, have ye?

ISHMAEL. He's sick, I'm told. But getting better.
ELIJAH.
Is he now? 'Morning to ye, shipmate—'morning.
Goin' aboard?

ISHMAEL.

Hands off, will ye?

ELIJAH.

'Morning to ye. . . .

Ain't goin' aboard, then?

ISHMAEL.

What's that to you?

ELIJAH.
'Morning to you, shipmate.
(ISHMAEL *starts away*.)

Shipped, have ye?
Name down on the papers? Well, what's signed is signed,
and what's to be will be; and then again
maybe it won't be quite. Anyhow it's fixed for
and arranged already, and there's got to be
some sailors go with him, I guess; God pity 'em!
'Morning to ye, shipmate!

ISHMAEL.

If you've anything
important, out with it! Or stop bamboozling—

ELIJAH. (*Cutting in.*)
I like to hear a man talk up that way—I like it.
You're just the man for him, the likes of you.

ISHMAEL.
If it's Cap'n Ahab you're referring to,
I've heard he's a good whale hunter—

ELIJAH.

That's true;

but better jump, shipmate; jump quick to his orders!
Step and growl,—growl and go's the word with Ahab.
ISHMAEL.
So I've heard.
ELIJAH.
                    Ye've heard that, have ye?
But nothing about that thing that happened to him
off Cape Horn, when Ahab lay like dead three days
and nights? Nothing about that deadly scrimmage
with the Spaniard, eh?—before the altar down in Santa?
Heard nothing about that, eh? Nor about the holy
silver calabash he spat into? Nor the leg—
the leg he lost according to the prophecy?
ISHMAEL.
Aye, I know all about the loss of Ahab's leg.
ELIJAH.
All about it,—*all?* Ye sure ye do?
ISHMAEL.
Pretty sure. And now, if you'll oblige me,—
ELIJAH.
                                                How?
ISHMAEL.
By stepping aside! I'm going to the Indian
and Pacific oceans and don't want to be detained.
ELIJAH.
Comin' back before breakfast? . . . Goodbye, to ye.
Shan't see you very soon, I guess; unless it be
before the Grand Jury. Sharp frost this morning, ain't it?
(*Exit* ELIJAH.)

(*SONG: A sea shanty, as the* SAILORS *aboard the "Pe-
    quod" bring up the anchor and prepare to sail.*)

PELEG.
Now, Mr. Starbuck—
STARBUCK.
                            Captain Peleg, aye?
PELEG.
Sure everything is right, eh? and nothing more

is needed from the shore? Well, call all hands, then,—
   muster
'em aft here, blast 'em!
   STARBUCK.
Aye, sir. But what of Captain Ahab?

(*The question makes* PELEG *uncomfortable. He gropes for
   a reply and blusters it out.*)

   PELEG.
                              Ahab?—
Ahab's ready. Muster all hands, Mr. Starbuck.
Aft here! ye sons of bachelors! Aft!
   STARBUCK.
All hands, Mr. Stubb.
   STUBB.
                    Aye, sir. (*Shouts as he goes.*)
                         All hands aft!
   STARBUCK.
I'd like to see our captain at least once, sir,
before we sail. . . .
   PELEG.
                    Don't think ye will, at present.
He keeps close inside the house,—a sort o' sick;
but not *sick*, either;—come aboard last night.
O, he's a queer man, Cap'n Ahab,
but a good one, too. A grand,
ungodly, god-like man—above the common.
Aye, Ahab's been in colleges,
as well as 'mongst the cannibals;
he's fixed his fiery lance in deadlier foes
n'whales. He's *Ahab*, man!—
The Bible Ahab, as ye know, was a crowned king.
   STARBUCK.
Aye, and a very vile one, Mister Peleg.
   PELEG.
What's that?
   STARBUCK.
            The Bible Ahab,—

when that wicked king was slain,
the dogs,—did they not lick his blood?

PELEG.

Don't ever speak those words again
on board the "Pequod"! No!
Don't say that anywhere!
Old Ahab didn't name himself.
I've sailed with him,—a mate like you,
and I know what he is:—a good man.
Not a pious good man, mebbe—
but a swearing good one.
Something, as ye'd say, like me!
only that there's more—much more of him.
Aye, aye, I know that on the passage home
he was—well, 'twas the bleeding stump
that brought that on . . . I know, too,
that ever since he lost that leg
last voyage by that cursed whale
he's been—well, been a kind o' moody—
savage sometimes. Aye. I know.
But that will all pass off.

STUBB. All hands are mustered, sir.

PELEG. Thankee, Mr. Stubb. (*Raising his voice to a
cheerful bellow.*) Now, then—ye misbegotten whale-
butchers! It'll be a short, cold Christmas for ye; but I
hope ye'll have fine weather soon, so Cap'n Ahab can be
moving out amongst ye— Ye harpooners, don't stove the
boats in needlessly—white cedar plank is raised full three
per cent this year!—Don't forget your prayers, either.—
Mr. Starbuck, mind ye don't keep the cheese too long
down in the hold, 'twill spoil, and cautious does it with
the butter— Butter's gone to twenty cents the pound.
Men—don't whale it too much o'Lord's days;—but don't
miss a fair chance either, that's rejecting Heaven's own
good gifts. Have an eye to the molasses, Mr. Stubb,—it's
a might leaky.—If ye touch at the islands, for God's
sake, Mr. Flask—beware of fornication!—Good luck to
ye all! And this day, three years from now, I'll have a

good hot smoking supper waitin' for ye all in old Nantucket!—God bless ye, and have ye in His holy keeping,
men!

(MUSIC.)

ISHMAEL.
Mister Peleg drops over the side
into the waiting boat. Our sails are set;
a screaming gull flies overhead;
we give three heavy-hearted cheers,
and blindly plunge, like fate,
into the lone Atlantic. . . .
(*MUSIC finishes.*)
For several days after we left Nantucket
nothing above hatches was seen of Captain Ahab.
The mates regularly relieved each other at the
    watches. . . .

(*The* THREE MATES *are together on the Forestage.*)

STARBUCK.
I don't much fancy shipping this way
to so long a voyage with a man I've never met. . . .
    ISHMAEL. (*Half introduction, half aside.*)
Starbuck, the chief mate—a Quaker by descent:
    STARBUCK. (*He stands with the other* MATES *but
speaks more or less to himself.*)
I suspect some wrong . . .
    STUBB. (*Briskly.*)
Well, wrong or right, we've got three years
before us to find out.
    ISHMAEL. (*As before.*)
                    Stubb is the second mate,—
good humoured, easy careless; taking perils as they come—
    STUBB.
I've heard whatever ship old Ahab sails in,
pays something extra for insurance policy.

(FLASK *laughs rather nervously at* STUBB'S *joke.*)

ISHMAEL.
The third mate, Flask,—of Tisbury in Martha's Vineyard;
a most pugnacious gentleman—concerning whales.
    FLASK. (*Sighs.*)
O, I've heard tales;—who knows—?
    STUBB.
                              Well,—be it what it will,
I'll go to it laughing, for a laugh's the easiest,
wisest way to all that's queer.

(*The* SAILORS *sing again. This time the shanty has a curi-
    ously savage ring, and under it there is a hint of
    MUFFLED DRUMS.*)

ISHMAEL.
The sailors:—Spaniards, Manxmen, Dutch,
Sicilian, Lascars and Icelandic—
picked and packed by some fatality
to sail our blessed whale-ship
from all sides of the seas,
and all the ends of earth.

Our tiger harpooneers:—
Queequeg, a tattooed island aboriginal;
the blood-skinned Iroquois Tashtego;
and great Daggoo, a giant, coal-black African. . . .

    (*SONG continues, DRUMS predominating.*)

STARBUCK.
O, God—to sail with such a heathen crew
that have small touch of mothers in them—!
    STUBB. (*With a twinkle.*)
Heathen, aye; but who can use a pious harpooneer?
Religion takes the shark out of 'em.
    FLASK.
Well, all aboard this ship seems pretty sharkish!

    (STUBB *joins him in a laugh.* SAILORS *are singing.*)

SAILORS.

Our captain stood upon the deck,
A spy-glass in his hand,
A viewing of those gallant whales
That blow at every strand,
O, your tubs in your boats, my boys,
And by your braces stand,
And we'll have one of those fine whales,
Hand boys, over hand!
So, be cheery, my lads! May your hearts never fail!
While the bold harpooner is striking the whale!

(*A pause.*)

STARBUCK.

Eight bells there, forward!

FLASK.

Eight bells there! D'ye hear, bell-boy? Strike the bell
    eight!

(*SHIP'S BELL strikes.*)

STUBB.

Eight bells there below! Tumble up!

ISHMAEL.

And there is also Pip, the cabin-boy; Black little Pip . . .
(THE YOUNG ACTRESS—*who will speak* PIP's *words—at
this lightly strikes a tambourine, without moving from
her post at the harmonium.*)
Poor Alabama boy, beating his tamborine . . .
(*Another light stroke of the tamborine.*)
Once cast adrift, tossed by the billows
'Till the whitecaps drove him mad,
now on the Pequod's forecastle
he chants his songs:

PIP. (*Singing.*)

    "Farewell and adieu to you, Spanish ladies!
    Farewell and adieu to you, ladies of Spain!"

A SAILOR.

Got it, Pip! Bang it, bell-boy!

PIP. (*Singing.*)
"Be cheery, my lads, may your hearts never fail
While the bold harpooner is striking the whale!"
(PIP'S *voice trails away at the end of the song.*)

(*A silence.*)

ISHMAEL. (*In a half-whisper.*)
There on the quarterdeck stood Captain Ahab. . . .
("THE GOVERNOR" *has moved into a circle of LIGHT,
he stands there motionless, and without speaking, in the
character of* AHAB. *After a pause.*)
Cut away from the stake, he looked;
wasted by fire; but not yet consumed.
Moody and stricken he stood before us,
with a crucifixion in his face. . . .

(*Another silence.*)

AHAB.
There are whales hereabouts—I smell 'em.
Look sharp for whales, all of ye! And if ye see
a white one—split your lungs for him!
(*After a moment he turns and moves away into the dark-
ness, the cane tapping on the wooden Stage floor like*
AHAB'S *ivory leg.*)
STUBB. (*Under his breath.*)
What d'ye think of that now, Mr. Starbuck?
Ain't there a small drop o' something queer
about that, eh?
FLASK.
                    A white whale—!
STUBB.
Did ye mark that? There's something special
in the wind. Stand by for it. . . .
STARBUCK.
                              I fear me that you're right.
Ahab has that that's bloody on his mind. . . .

(*LIGHT change. A low sighing of WIND in the shrouds.*)

ISHMAEL.
Turning to eastward, the Cape winds began;
(*WIND louder.*)
They howled round us and we rose and fell
upon long, troubled seas. . . .

(*The SHIP'S BELL is heard.*)

THE STAGE MANAGER. (*Speaking the words as an announcement.*) "Midnight, Forecastle—Harpooneers and Sailors . . . lounging and lying in various attitudes, all singing in chorus. . . ."

(*During this last the* ACTORS *have grouped themselves at one side of the Stage.*)

ACTORS. (*Sing "Sailors' Song."*)
    We'll drink tonight with hearts as light,
    To love, as gay and fleeting
    As bubbles that swam, on the breaker's brim
    And break on the lips while meeting!
THE STAGE MANAGER. "French sailor— Hist, boys! Let's have a jig or two. What say ye? Pip—little Pip— your tambourine!" (*Change of tone.*) "Pip—sulky and sleepy—'Don't know where it is.' "
THE YOUNG ACTRESS. (*Repeating the line "in character."*) Don't know where it is.
THE STAGE MANAGER. "Beat thy belly, then, and wag thy ears! Jig it, men, I say. Damn me, won't you dance? . . . Maltese Sailor: 'Where's your girls?'—"

(*WIND louder.*)

AN ACTOR. (*Picking up the line.*) Where's your girls? Who but a fool would take his left hand by his right, and say to himself, how d'ye do? Partners! I need partners!
THE STAGE MANAGER. "Azore Sailor—"
ANOTHER ACTOR. (*"In character."*)
It's the snow-caps turn to jig now.

They'll shake their tassels soon!
I wish the waves were women:
I'd go drown and dance with 'em!

THE STAGE MANAGER. (*Still reading.*) "Women . . .
swift glances of the warm, wild bosoms in the dance, and
over-arboring arms hiding such ripe and bursting grapes!"

ANOTHER ACTOR. "Sicilian Sailor—" (*Then "in character.*") —fleet interlacings of the limbs—lithe swayings
—coyings—flutterings! Lip! Heart! All graze—eh, pagan?

ANOTHER. "Tahitian Sailor—" Hail, holy nakedness
of our dancing girls!—The Heeva-Heeva! Low-veiled,
high palmed Tahiti!

THE STAGE MANAGER. How the sea rolls swashing
'gainst the side! (*The LIGHTS dim; the WIND rises.
Then, on the other side of the Stage,* AHAB *is discovered.*)
"Captain Ahab in his cabin, a wrinkled roll of sea-charts
spread before him on the screwed-down table."

(*MUSIC: the harmonium—actually by now, the electric
    organ—provides here a very faint and weird musical
    color by way of background.*)

ISHMAEL.
With charts of all four of the oceans,
Ahab threads a maze of currents,
eddies and the sets of tides.
He calculates the drifting
of the sperm-whale's food, not only
at substantiated times, upon the well-known
feeding-grounds does Ahab look
to find his prey, but also, by his art,
crossing the great areas between
those grounds he can so place himself
as even then not to be wholly
without prospect of a meeting.

But in this broad and boundless ocean
can he hope to find one solitary
and particular whale?

AHAB. (*Looking up from his charts.*)
Have I not tallied him? His fins
are bored and scalloped like a lost
sheep's ear—and shall he then escape?
Escape?—I'll chase him round Good Hope,
and round the Horn, and round the Norway
Maelstrom! Aye, round perdition's flames,
before I'll give him up!
(*THUNDER.*)
The lightning flashes through my skull!
Mine eye-balls ache and my whole beaten
brain seems rolling on a stunning ground!
I am the bloody man! And I will have revenge!

(*THUNDER again. LIGHT change. The WIND steadily
rising.*)

THE STAGE MANAGER. (*Reading.*) Danish Sailor:
"Crack! Crack, old ship!"
AN ACTOR. Old Manx Sailor: "How the three pines
shake!"

(*THUNDER.*)

ISHMAEL.
Thick in our rear fly the inscrutable
sea-ravens . . . and heaves, and heaves, unrestingly
heaves the black sea, as if its vast tides
were a conscience: the great mundane soul
in anguish,—anguish and remorse . . .

(*All the noises of the growing STORM are louder.*)

THE STAGE MANAGER. "Midnight—The Forecastle
Bulwarks. Stubb and Flask mounted on them, and pass-
ing additional lashings over the anchors—"
STUBB. (*In a cheerful shout.*)
Seems to me as if we're lashing down these anchors
now, as if we never thought to have a need

for dropping 'em again! I wonder, Flask—
Is the world anchored anywheres?

    FLASK. Well, Stubb—if she is, she swings with a long-ish cable!

(THUNDER. LIGHTS brighten on AHAB's *cabin.* STAR-
   BUCK *approaches him.)*

    STARBUCK. *(Breathlessly.)*
The main-top-sail yards, sir—we must send it down!
(Bent over his charts, AHAB *makes no reply.)*
The band's working loose, and the lee left's half stranded!
(Still no answer.)
Shall I strike it, sir?
    AHAB.
Strike nothing: lash it.
    STARBUCK.
Sir! In God's name—! *Sir!*
    AHAB.
Strike nothing! *(Rises.)*
By masts and keels! Ye take me
for the hunchback skipper of some coasting
smack? Mr. Starbuck, send everybody aft.

(THUNDER, WIND.)

    STARBUCK.
But, Cap'n Ahab! In a blow like this—!
    AHAB.
Mr. Starbuck—muster all hands aft.

(A pause. They eye each other.)

    STARBUCK.
Aye, sir.

(THUNDER. As STARBUCK *starts away, the LIGHTS
   shift to* STUBB.)*

STUBB. (*Singing.*)

> "Oh, jolly is the gale,
> And a joker is the whale,
> A'flourishing his tail,
> Such a gamy, jesty, hoky-poky lad's
> the Ocean, oh!"

PIP'S VOICE. (*Out of the darkness.*)
Crish, crash! There goes the jib-stay! Hold on hard!
Jimini, what a squall!

STUBB. (*Singing.*)

> "Thunder splits the ships,
> But he only smacks his lips—"

STARBUCK. (*Hurrying up.*) All hands, aft, Stubb, Captain's orders. (*Cupping his hands and shouting up.*) Masthead's there! Come down!

(*Cries of "Aye!" from the surrounding darkness; FIGURES are seen gathering.*)

A SAILOR. What's that I saw—lightning?
ANOTHER. No; Daggoo showing his teeth.

(*Nervous laughter.*)

DAGGOO. White skin, white liver!

(*A scuffling fight starts and is almost instantly broken up by* STUBB *and* STARBUCK.)

STARBUCK. Avast there!
STUBB. (*Under his breath.*) Here's the Cap'n!

(*The* FIGHTERS *break, and* ALL *fall back as* AHAB *steps into the light.*)

AHAB. Thank ye, Mr. Starbuck.

(*A pause.*)

PIP'S VOICE.
O, big white God up high there in the dark!
have mercy on this small black boy down here;
preserve me from all men that hasn't bowels
for feeling fear!

AHAB. What d'ye do when you see a whale, men? (*A
short silence, then* AHAB *suddenly repeats the question in
a great roar.*) *What d'ye do when ye see a whale?*

A SAILOR. Sing out for him!

ANOTHER SAILOR. Aye, Cap'n—sing out loud!

AHAB. Sing out for him, d'ye? (*Murmurs of "Aye! Aye,
Cap'n!"*) And what d'ye do next, men?

SAILOR. Lower away.

ANOTHER. Lower away and after him!

(*Excited shouts—"After him!"*)

AHAB. And what tune is it, ye pull to, men?

THIRD SAILOR. A dead whale or a stove boat!

AHAB. Aye, that's the tune!

(*The cry is repeated in chorus: "A dead whale or a stove
boat!"*)

MASTHEADERS. Aye, Cap'n Ahab? Aye?

AHAB. Look ye—d'ye see this ounce o' Spanish Gold?
(ALL *are suddenly silent as* AHAB *holds up before them
the big, bright coin.*) A sixteen dollar gold-piece, men!
Y'see it? Hand me a top-maul, Mr. Starbuck, and I'll
fix this Spanish gold-piece to the mast. (*Eager shouts.*)
Steward—draw us the great measure o' grog! (*Delighted
reaction.* AHAB *hammers the coin to the mast with three
heavy blows, then turns back to the crew.*)
Whoever of ye raises me
a white-headed whale—*white*,
mind ye—with a wrinkled brow
and a great crooked jaw; whoever
raises me that whale—with three
holes punctured in his starboard fluke—

Whoever of ye raises me that same white whale—
he gets this big gold ounce, my boys!
(*A cheer goes up; much happy jabbering as the* STEWARD
distributes grog, but this abruptly breaks off as AHAB
raises a hand for silence.)
A white whale,—*white!* Mastheaders,—
skin your eyes for him! Look sharp
for white water!

TASHTEGO.
                    Cap'n Ahab—?

AHAB. Aye, Tashtego?

TASHTEGO. That whale—?

AHAB. Aye, my sweet cannibal?

TASHTEGO. This here *white* whale—

AHAB. Aye, aye, my lovely man-eater? What is it,
Tash?

TASHTEGO.
Is it the old white one *hisself?*
The one that some calls—Moby Dick?

AHAB. (*With a great shout, triumphantly.*) *Moby
Dick!* (*The excited murmuring of the* SAILORS *breaks
off at the vehemence of this cry. A short silence, then*
AHAB *speaks almost in a whisper.*) Ye know the *white*
whale, then?

TASHTEGO. (*In a hoarse, half-whisper.*)
Do he fan-tail a little curious,
sir,—before he go down?

DAGGOO.
Have he a curious spout, too,—
bushy, very bushy—even for a parmacetty?
And mighty quick, too, Cap'n Ahab?

QUEEQUEG.
An' have he one—two—three—
oh, good many iron in him hide, too,
Cap'n?—all twiskee-tee-be-twisk—

AHAB.
                                        Corkscrew!
Aye, Queequeg! Harpoons lie all twisted
up and wrenched in him; and aye, Daggoo—

his spout's a big one, like a shock
o'wheat, and white as our Nantucket wool;
aye, Tash, he fan-tails like a split jib
in a squall. Death and devils, men—!
It's Moby Dick ye've seen!—*Moby Dick!*

(*The voices of the* SAILORS *have been rising with the rising noises of the STORM. There is a tone now almost of terror.*)

STARBUCK.
Captain, I too have heard of Moby Dick.
Was it not Moby Dick that took away your leg?

(*A sudden silence.*)

AHAB.
Aye, Mr. Starbuck,—aye. I met him once.
Aye, it was Moby Dick dismasted me;
Moby Dick that brought me down to this
dead stump I stand on now. Aye, aye—
it was that cursed white whale
that razed me; made a peggin' lubber
o' me to the end o' time—
(*More silence. Suddenly* AHAB *yells.*)
That's what ye've shipped for, men!
Ye've shipped to chase the white whale
over every sea until he spouts black blood!
(*THUNDER.*)
What d'ye say, men—?
(*The THUNDER dies away. Silence again.*)
Will ye splice hands on it?
(*The uneasy* SAILORS *stand motionless.*)
Pass the grog again, and double measure!
(*A pleased muttering at this, which grows as the* STEWARD *hurries among the* SAILORS *ladling out more drink.*)
What's the long face for, Mr. Starbuck?
(*Shouting.*)
Drink and pass!

(*"Drink and pass!" is echoed in chorus.*)
Long swallows, men!
It's hot as Satan's hoof, it spiralizes in ye!
(*Laughter.*)
Spiralizes!—forks out at the serpent snapping eye!
What say ye, men—? A sharp eye for the white whale!
   SAILORS. (*Half-drunk.*)
Aye, aye! A sharp eye for the whale—!

(*THUNDER.*)

TASHTEGO.
A sharp lance for him—for Moby Dick!

(*Wild SHOUTS at this.*)

AHAB.
Well, Mr. Starbuck?
Will ye not chase the white whale with the rest
of us? Are ye not game for Moby Dick?
   STARBUCK.
I'm game for his crook'd jaw, Cap'n—
and for the jaws of death, too,—
if it comes fairly in the way of business.
   AHAB. (*Repeating the words with contempt.*)
In the way of business—!
   STARBUCK.
But I signed articles to hunt whales,
not my commander's vengeance!
How many barrels, Cap'n, will your vengeance
yield ye, if ye get it? How much
will vengeance fetch in the Nantucket market?
   AHAB.
Come closer, Mr. Starbuck—if money
be the measurer, if the accountants
have computed their great counting-house
the globe by girdling it all with guineas
one to every three parts of an inch,—
then let me tell thee that my vengeance

will fetch me a premium—here!
(*He strikes his chest.*)
   STARBUCK.
Vengeance on a poor dumb brute that struck
thee blindly, out of instinct? Vengeance
on a poor dumb thing!—it's blasphemy!
Ahab, beware of Ahab!—beware of thyself, old man!
   AHAB.
He tasks me, Mr. Starbuck!—
Tasks and heaps me! I see in him
outrageous strength, malice inscrutable;
that thing inscrutable I chiefly hate,—
and be the white whale agent or be he
principal—I'll wreak that hate
upon him! Talk not to me of blasphemy;
I'd strike the sun if it insulted me!
(*Wheeling back to the drunken crew.*)
Drink, ye harpooneers! Drink and swear—
Swear death to Moby Dick!
   ALL. (*Repeating the great roar.*)
                          Death to Moby Dick!
   AHAB.
If we hunt not Moby Dick, God hunt us all.
   STARBUCK. (*Aside.*)
God keep us all!

        (*The Stage goes DARK. THUNDER.*)

   ISHMAEL.
I, Ishmael, was of that crew.
My oath was welded with the rest.

Our souls were so possessed that Ahab's hate
was almost ours, and the white whale
our foe as much as his. How all this
came to be, or how—that grey-headed
ungodly, bad old man might seem to us
the gliding demon of the seas of life—
all this to explain would be to dive
far deeper than Ishmael can go.

(*LIGHT comes up on* AHAB. *He is near the place on the Stage which represents his cabin.*)

AHAB.
'Twas not too hard a task:
my one cogged circle fits their various
wheels . . . and they revolve. . . .
(*With a sudden change of tone.*)
But what's that Starbuck said?
Ahab—beware of Ahab!

(*On the other side of the Stage LIGHT now reveals* STARBUCK.)

STARBUCK.
My soul is more than matched;
she's over-manned . . . he drilled down deep
and blasted reason out of me. . . .
 AHAB.
I'll go below . . . below . . .

Down to a tomb—it's very like—
for an old Cap'n to descend this narrow scuttle
to his grave-dug bed. I seek my nightly rest
'tween shrouds, and down I go, gripping
the iron banisters to help my crippled way.
Hark to the crack and din of Ahab's bony step!
My dreams'll be of the crunching teeth of shark. . . .

(FLASK *and* STUBB *are revealed; like* AHAB *and* STARBUCK *they occupy a separate area of LIGHT.*)

FLASK.
If his leg were cut off at the hip, now—
clear to at the hip, 'twould be a different thing.
But Ahab has a *knee*.
 STUBB. (*Cutting him off.*)
I don't know that, my little man.
I never saw him kneel.

(*In the "cabin"* AHAB *seats himself in his chair.*)

AHAB.
Old age is wakeful; the longer linked
with life the less man has to do
with aught that looks like death.
    STUBB.
Ain't in his bed now either, but three hours
out o' twenty-four. Didn't the steward
tell me of a morning he always finds
the old man's hammock clothes all rumpled up
and tumbled, and the sheets down at the foot,
the coverlid tied almost into knots,
and the pillow sort o' frightful hot—
like a baked brick had been on it,—
A hot old man!
    FLASK.
                    I guess he's got
what some folks call a conscience.
    STUBB.
Well, well—I don't know what it is;
but Lord keep me from catching it!

(*The LIGHT goes from* STUBB *and* FLASK. *Now only*
    AHAB *and* STARBUCK *are shown; on opposite sides*
    of the Stage.)

AHAB.
I leave a white and turbid wake:
Pale waters, paler cheeks where'er I sail. . . .
    STARBUCK.
Horrible old man!
He broods there in his sternward cabin
over the dead water of the wake,
and hunted by its wolfish gurglings. . . .
Whose thinking thus makes him Prometheus;
a vulture feeds upon that heart forever:—
that vulture the very creature he creates.

AHAB.

Is then the crown too heavy that I wear?
'Tis iron, I know—not gold; split, too—
the jagged edge is galling, and my brain
beats against solid metal—!
The diver sun, slow dived from noon
goes down. My sooul mounts up, yet wearies
with her endless hill! Time was,
when, as the sunset spurred me, so
the sunset soothed. No more. No more.
This lovely light it lights not me.
Damned—most subtly and malignantly,
damned in the midst of paradise!

STARBUCK. (*In a whisper.*)

I think I see his end,
but feel that I must help him to it. . . .

AHAB.

There was a prophecy that I should be
dismembered; and aye!—I've lost this leg.
I now do prophecy that I'll dismember
my dismemberer!

STARBUCK.

                      . . . a fatal end
that I must help him to. Yet will I try
to fight ye, ye grim phantom futures!

AHAB.

What I've dared I've willed;
and what I've willed I'll do!
I laugh at ye, great bully gods!
No. No, ye've knocked me down,
but I am up again! Ahab's compliments
to ye!—come see if you can swerve me.—
Swerve me? The path to my fixed purpose
is laid down with iron rails. Swerve me?
Over unsounded gorges, through the rifled
hearts of mountains, under torrents beds
unerringly I rush! Swerve me?—

STARBUCK.

O God! Stand by me, bind me, hold me!

AHAB.
Stern all! The white whale spouts thick blood!

(The only LIGHT is on AHAB, *and this is rapidly dimming, as:)*

THE CURTAIN FALLS

ACT TWO

*After the interval—when the house lights have been
dimmed and the auditorium is in darkness—a voice is
heard calling out from the back of the theatre:*

VOICE OF THE "BACHELOR." Ahoy the "Pequod"—
"Pequod" ahoy!

(*The CURTAIN rises.*)

VOICE OF THE "PEQUOD'S" MASTHEAD.
Sail ho!—sail ho!
STARBUCK. (*Calling up to the* MASTHEAD.)
Where away?
MASTHEAD.
Three points to the starboard bow, sir,
and bringing down the breeze to us!

(*Enter* AHAB.)

VOICE OF THE "BACHELOR."
Ahoy the "Pequod"! This is the "Bachelor,"
A whaling-ship out of New Bedford.
Come aboard!
AHAB. (*Cupping his hands and shouting.*)
Have ye seen the white whale?
VOICE OF THE "BACHELOR."
Come aboard! and have a glass with us!
AHAB.
Seen the white whale?
VOICE OF THE "BACHELOR."
No, only heard of him; but don't believe in him, at all!
AHAB.
Lost any men?
VOICE OF THE "BACHELOR."
No, not to speak of—

44

Two islanders, that's all. But come aboard, old hearty!
We'll take that black look from your brow!
Come on aboard, for we're a full ship, homeward bound!
  AHAB.
A full ship homeward bound, eh!
Call me an empty ship, and outward bound!
Forward there! Set sail all, Mr. Starbuck, and keep
her to the wind!
  VOICE OF THE "BACHELOR."
Just one half hour—
  AHAB. (*Cutting him off.*)
Up helm! Keep her off round the world!

(*MUSIC.*)

  ISHMAEL.
Were this round world an endless plain,
by sailing eastward we could reach
new distances forever; forever find
new sights more sweet and strange than any Cyclades or
Islands of King Solomon.
But in pursuit of mysteries;
or in tormented hunting of that demon phantom
that swims before all human hearts
whilst chasing such across the globe,
they lead us on in barren mazes,
or midway leave us whelmed. . . .

(*MUSIC: transition. A change of LIGHTS.*)

  ISHMAEL.
Months passed, and under easy sail, the ivory "Pequod"
swept across four separate cruising grounds.
One silent night a silvery jet was seen
far in advance of the white bubbles at the bow.
Lit by the moon, it looked celestial;
some plumed and glittering god uprising from the sea.
  MASTHEAD.
There she blows!

(*MUSIC*.)

AHAB.

Mr. Starbuck.

STARBUCK.

Aye, Cap'n Ahab?

AHAB.

Set t'gallants and royals. Spread the stunsails.

STARBUCK.

Aye, Cap'n Ahab.

ISHMAEL.

The silvery jet was no more seen that night,
Each sailor swore he saw it once, but not a second time.

This mid-night spout had almost grown a thing forgotten,
when, some days after, lo! at the same silent hour—

MASTHEAD.

There she blows!

(*MUSIC again*.)

ISHMAEL.

And so, night after night it served us
vanishing again—and lo!
after two nights or three
advancing ever further in our van
the solitary jet allured us on.

Some of our seamen swore
whenever we described the spout
'twas always cast by one whale,
and that whale Moby Dick.

THE STAGE MANAGER. "The deck—first night watch
. . . the ship's carpenter standing before his vice-bench
busily fitting the ivory joists for Ahab's new leg."

CARPENTER. Oh, he's a hard driver is Cap'n Ahab!
Driven one leg to death, and now wears out bone legs by
the cord! . . . (*Continues working*.) Time—if I ever
had time I'd turn him out as neat a leg now as ever—
(*Sneezes*.) —scraped to a fine lady in a parlour. (*Sneezes
again*.) Drat the file and drat the bone! 'Twon't let me

speak. This is what an old fella gits fur workin' in old
lumber! Dust . . . amputate a live bone, now, and ye
don't git it. . . .

(*He stops, hearing the "tap-tap" of* AHAB's *approach.
The little black boy,* PIP, *is following.*)

PIP.
Cap'n—Cap'n—Cap'n master Ahab—!
Here's little Pip, trying to get on board again!
  AHAB.
Lad, lad . . .
Thou must not follow Ahab now.
(*To the* CARPENTER.)
Well, man-maker?
  CARPENTER.
Just in time, sir. If the Cap'n pleases,
I'll just mark out the length—
  PIP.
You've not your body whole, sir!
do you but use poor me for your lost leg.
  AHAB.
I tell thee no, it cannot be.
  PIP.
Just tread upon me, sir, I ask no more—
  CARPENTER.
Avast there, crazy little loon!
  AHAB.
Hands off that holiness! Well, Pip—
  PIP.
Pip's missing: jumped from the whale-boat!
Have you fished him up here, fishermen?
It drags hard . . . for he's holding on. Cut him—
cut him away! We haul no cowards here!
  AHAB.
Where say'st thou little Pip was, lad?
  PIP.
There's his arm—there! breaking water!
Give us a hatchet, carpenter! and cut it off!

CARPENTER. (*With elaborate patience.*)
Just stand here, sir; I'll get the measure—
AHAB.
Measure? Well, it's not for the first time.
While you're about it, carpenter,
I'll order a new man, a complete man,
after a more desirable pattern.
Imprimis, fifty feet high in his socks,
legs with roots to 'em to stay in one place;
No heart at all, and eyes—
No, put a skylight on the top of the head.

(*The* CARPENTER, *with a nervous laugh, begins sawing.*)

PIP.
One hundred pounds of clay reward for Pip!
Pip—not so tall—looks cowardly—
best known by that! Ding! Ding! Black Pip!
Who has seen Pip the coward?
AHAB.
Are there no hearts above the snow line?
O, ye frozen heaven! Look down here—
ye did beget this luckless child,
and have abandoned him, creative libertines!
(*To the* CARPENTER.)
What are you sneezing for?
CARPENTER.
Bone's kind of dusty, sir.
AHAB.
Take the hint then;
when you're dead, don't bury yourself
under living people's noses.
PIP.
There—there astern—!
AHAB.
How does it feel to drown, lad?
PIP.
To drown? I gushed into the sea!
My soul flew from my mouth!

See—there it bobs along, and nobody—
nobody to heed it! A coiled fish
brushed against me. Hello! this is death, said I,
Maybe it were death, Cap'n, but it wouldn't heed me.

(AHAB *stares at him for a moment then turns back to the*
CARPENTER.)

AHAB.
Would it speak well for your work, Carpenter,
if, when I come to mount this new leg,
in the identical place with it,
I feel another?—my old, lost leg
of flesh and bone?
    CARPENTER.
True, Cap'n, I've heard tell
o' somethin' curious on that score.
They do say a dismasted man
don't ever quite entirely get rid
o' feeling his first spar.
    AHAB.
Look, put your live leg here—
here in the place where mine was—
so—here is now only one,
a single distinct leg to any eye.
Hist—how d'ye know that some
entire, living, thinking thing
may not invisibly be standing
there, where you are standing?
In your most solitary hours, then
don't you ever fear the feel of eavesdroppers?
    CARPENTER. (*Half to himself.*)
Good Lord above!
    AHAB. (*With a brusque change of tone.*)
How long before the new leg's done?
    CARPENTER.
An hour, sir; mebbe; mebbe more.
    AHAB.
Here I am, as proud as a Greek God,

yet debtor to this blockhead
for a bone to stand on!
I, who'd be free as air yet owe
for the flesh in the tongue I brag with. . . .

(*The* CARPENTER *goes.* PIP *seizes* AHAB'S *hands.*)

PIP.

What's this?

Here's velvet sharkskin. Ah, now
had poor Pip felt so kind a thing as this
perhaps he'd never have been lost!
Sir, let the ship's carpenter come now
and rivet these two hands together;
the black one with the white;
I will not let this go. . . .
  AHAB.
Oh, boy, nor will I thee; unless I'd drag thee
to worse horrors than are here.
Come! I feel prouder
leading thee by thy black hand,
than though I grasped an Emperor's!
Come to my cabin, lad. . . .
  PIP. (*Still clinging to* CAPTAIN'S *hand as they enter
the cabin.*)
I will not sink—
  AHAB.
No, lad, you're tied to me.
  PIP.

Hang on, Pip!

  AHAB.
Tied to me with cords, lad—woven of my heart strings.
Yet the hour is coming when old Ahab
might well scare thee from him.
There's that in thee to curing my malady.

(*A silence.*)

  PIP. (*Murmuring to himself.*)
Alas, for all my drowning in that snowy foam,

my living skin's still black. . . .
(*He weeps.*)
   AHAB.
Weep so, and I'll murder thee. . . .
Beware . . . Ahab's too mad . . .
   PIP.
Master—if the current carry you, far off
to those sweet Antilles where the beaches
beat with water-flowers—will ye do
a favour for me, master? Seek out Pip,
black Pip, who's missing long—
I think he's in those far Antilles—
Find him; comfort him; he must be very sad;
for look!—he's left his hand behind!
(*Holds up his hand.*)
I found it, and how black it is—
how black for all its washing . . .
   AHAB.
Blackness . . . whiteness . . . as though a man
who's white is anything more dignified
than a white-washed negro.
   PIP.
My bones, my bones are white, sir.
   AHAB.
Dost thou know aught, lad, of the whiteness of the whale?
   PIP.
The white whale . . . Moby Dick's the name . . .
   AHAB.
Aye, but the *whiteness* of him—
(*MUSIC.*)
Whiteness, lad, enhances many things:
marble and japonica and pearls;
the innocence of brides; the ermine
majesty of justice. Yet something lurks
in whiteness strikes panic to the soul!
   PIP.
The waves was foaming white
when I was drowning, master;
I was terrible afraid. . . .

AHAB.
Whiteness, terror . . .

Even the King of Terror
rides his pallid horses; and think thee
of the albatross, whence come those clouds
of dread in which the snowy phantom sails
in all imaginations. And what is it
in the Albino man so strangely shocks
the eye, that he is loathed by his own kin?
It is the whiteness which invests him!
    PIP.
Whiteness . . . and ghosts . . .
and ghosts are white . . .
    AHAB.
Ghosts, riding in a milk-white fog . . .
the muffled rollings of the milky sea;
bleak rustlings of the festooned frosts
of mountains; and the desolate shiftings
of the windrowed snows of prairies . . .

Pondering all this, the palsied universe
lies white before us like a leper.

And of whiteness—all of whiteness—
the Albino whale has been my symbol!
D'ye wonder at my fiery hunt?

                (*The MUSIC ends. A silence.*)

    PIP.
Death to whiteness!
    AHAB. (*Very gently.*)
Abide here in my cabin, lad,
and they shall serve thee, as if thou
wert the captain, in the captain's chair!
Be thou like me.
    PIP.
Good master!
    AHAB.
Ahab's cabin is Pip's home—while Ahab lives.

And now I quit thee . . . thou'lt hear my ivory foot
upon the deck and know I'm near to thee.
So God forever bless thee;
and—if it come to that—God save thee,
let what will befall.

(*He goes.* PIP *is left alone.*)

PIP.
Here he in this instant stood;
I stand in his air,—but now I'm all alone.
Where's Pip? Stay here—he said.
Aye, and he told me this screwed chair
was mine. Here then I'll seat me,
'gainst the transom, in the ship's full middle,
all her keel and her three masts afore me. . . .

Here great admirals sometimes sits at table . . .
and lord it over rows of captains and lieutenants!
Fill up, gentlemens, with your gold lace!
Gentlemens—have ye seen one Pip?—
a little negro lad, hang-dog look
and cowardly? Jumped from a whale-boat once;
let's drink shame upon all cowards!
I name no names! Shame upon 'em.
Hist!

        I hear ivory—oh, master! master!
walk on, walk over me, but here I'll stay.

Aye, through the stern strike rocks;
and they bulge through; and oysters
come to join me!

If only Pip was here, I could endure it. . . .
Where's Pip . . . Ding-dong!

(*The LIGHT goes from the cabin, and comes up on the
    deck, where* AHAB—*as we have heard from the steady
    "tap-tapping" of his bone leg during* PIP'S *last speech
    —is steadily pacing.* STUBB *approaches* AHAB, *his*

manner embarrassed. He is trying to make a respect-
ful joke out of a difficult request.)

STUBB.
Cap'n Ahab, sir . . . evening to ye.
   AHAB.
Mr. Stubb?
   STUBB.
Well, Cap'n, for three hours now, almost a whole watch,
you've walked the night away up here on deck—
and decks are only plank, sir; you'll excuse me,
and we poor sleepy chaps below, Cap'n—
our hammocks are a bare few inches, sir,
under that promenading ivory heel.
If I might be so bold, sir, to suggest
some class o' muffler—or maybe Chips
can figger somethin' in the line of padding, sir—
could be a ball of tow, or—
   AHAB.
A ball of tow! Am I a cannon-ball? Would ye wad me?
Go below!
   STUBB.

        But, sir—

   AHAB.

              Below, below!
Back to your nightly grace, where such as you
sleep between shrouds. Down dog and kennel!
   STUBB.
I'm not used to be spoken to that way, sir—
   AHAB.
Avast!
   STUBB.
No, sir, not yet. I will not tamely be called a dog, sir.
   AHAB.
Then be called ten times a donkey; and a mule, an ass!
Be gone before I clear the world of ye!

(STUBB *makes an almost involuntary move towards*
    AHAB, *then stops—held in the old man's gaze. A*

pause. Then STUBB *turns away. The SHIP'S BELL is heard.* AHAB *is now a silhouette as* STUBB *moves into LIGHT on the fore-stage.*)

STUBB.
I was never served before so
without giving back a hard blow for it. . . .
Queer . . . somehow, I don't know
whether to go back and strike him—or—
go down here on my knees and pray for him!
It's queer . . . he's queer. . . . Aye, take him fore and
    aft,
he's just about the queerest old man
Stubb has ever sailed with.
    VOICE OF A SHIP. (*As before, from the back of the auditorium.*)
Ahoy, the "Pequod"!

(*MUSIC. A murmur and a bustle of movement as the* CREW *gathers to hail the passing ship.*)

    ISHMAEL.
A large ship is described, the "Rachel"
bearing directly down upon the "Pequod,"
all her spars clustering with men.
    VOICE OF THE "RACHEL."
Ahoy, the "Pequod"!
    FLASK. (*Aside to* STUBB.)
Bad news. There's bad news from that ship.
Just mark me.
    AHAB.
                Ahoy, the "Rachel"!
Have ye seen the white whale?
    VOICE OF THE "RACHEL."
                        Aye, yesterday.
But have *you* seen a whale-boat?
    AHAB.
                        Yesterday? . . .

Voice of the "Rachel."
Adrift—a whale-boat—a drifting whale-boat—
Ahab.
Where was he—? Where?—
Voice of the "Rachel."
The whale-boat—it's a—
Ahab. (*Cutting in.*)
Moby Dick, ye fool!
Where d'ye raise him? *Where?*
Voice of the "Rachel."
We were engaging with a shoal of parmacetty—
Our fourth boat raised a great white hump
some miles to leeward, and gave chase.
Ahab.
Not killed? *Not killed?*
Voice of the "Rachel."
This boat of ours, after a keen sail
before the wind seemed to have fastened,
though the most we saw was bubbling
white water and then nothing—nothing.
The white whale must have run off, several miles
with our boat on the line. Night came;
we crowded sail; every man of us aloft
on lookout; yet not the least glimpse
of the missing keel was seen!
Stubb. (*Aside to* Flask.)
Who ever heard of two whale ships to pause
and cruise about after one little boat?
Flask.
Not in the whaling season!
Voice of the "Rachel."
My boy! My own son is among them!
For God's sake let me charter you—
Just eight and forty hours; I'll pay—
I'll pay ye roundly for it!
Stubb.
His son!—'tis his son he's lost!
Now what says Ahab? We must save that boy.

VOICE OF THE "RACHEL."
But eight and forty hours!—my only son—
not twelve years old—I'll pay ye anything!
(*A pause. The* CREW *turns expectantly towards* AHAB.
He stands motionless.)
I will not go 'till you say *aye* to me. . . .
    AHAB.
Brace forward, Mr. Starbuck;
let the ship sail as before.

(*A low angry murmur from the "Pequod's"* CREW. *Furi-
ous cries from the distant "Rachel."*)

VOICE OF THE "RACHEL."
You have a child too, Ahab— Do to me
as you would have me do to you
in a like case—! Run, men,
stand by to square in yards.

(*The* CREW *starts into motion as though obeying the an-
guished command from across the water, but* AHAB'S
voice freezes them.)

    AHAB.
Touch not a rope yarn!
(*Calling out.*)
                I lose time
Your boy was drowned, man, with the rest of 'em.
God bless ye—may I forgive myself—
Masthead! skin your eyes! brace forward there!
(*Quietly and fervently to himself.*)
He's in these seas. . . .
Somewhere in these seas, old Moby Dick is swim-
    ming. . . .
    ISHMAEL.
Soon the two ships diverge their wakes
we see the "Rachel" yaw, thither and hither,
at every spot, however small,
upon the sea. Her masts and yards

all are thick clustered with her men,
as three tall cherry trees
when boys are cherrying along the boughs.
This ship that so weeps with the spray,
remains still, without comfort.
The "Rachel" mourning for her children. . . .

(*The MUSIC finishes. A short pause. Then* THE STAGE
    MANAGER *speaks.*)

  THE STAGE MANAGER.
"Scene—the after deck—
Ahab—later Starbuck.
A fair morning—"
  ISHMAEL.
The feminine air has gentle thoughts:
the snow white wings of speckled birds
and in the deeps: mighty Leviathan
the gentle giant squid, swordfish and shark;
these the untroubled murderous
thinkings of the masculine sea.
Tied up; twisted; eyes like coals
still glowing in the ashes of a ruin,
Ahab lifts up to the clearness of the morn
his splintered helmet of a brow.

This glad, this happy air, this winsome sky
at last seems almost to dissolve
the canker wrinkled beating in his heart
the cruel step-mother world
now throws affectionate arms
around that stubborn neck.

Old Ahab drops a tear into the sea
nor does the vast Pacific hold such wealth
as that one drop. . . .

(STARBUCK *has come into the scene and now approaches*
    AHAB.)

AHAB.
Starbuck—
  STARBUCK.
Sir.
  AHAB.
Starbuck, it's a mild, mild wind.
And a mild-looking sky. On such a day—
very much a sweetness such as this—
I struck my first whale, Starbuck,
a boy harpooner of eighteen.
Forty years continual whaling, Starbuck—
forty years away, away—whole oceans—
from that young girl whom I wedded,
sailing from Cape Horn next day
and leaving in my marriage pillow
one small dent. O, Starbuck
what a forty years fool—fool—
old fool has Ahab been! Tell me,
do I look so old, so very old?

I feel most deadly faint, and bowed,
and humped, as though I were old Adam
staggering beneath the piled up centuries
since Paradise! Close! Stand close
to me and let me look into a human eye. . . .
It's better than an empty sea
or the blank sky; this is the magic
glass, man; I see my wife and child
there in your eye. . . . Starbuck, lower not
when I do! Lower not when branded Ahab
would give chase to Moby Dick!
Not with my far-off home there, in your eye!
  STARBUCK.
Oh, my captain! captain! Grand old heart!
Why should you or anyone give chase
to that damned hated fish?
Let's fly these deadly waters! Let us home!

Alter the course, let me—
How cheerfully then, my captain,

We'll bowl our way to old Nantucket!
I think, sir, they have some such mild blue days,
even as this, back in Nantucket.
  AHAB.
They have, they have, I've seen 'em!
Some summer days in the morning.
About this time—yes, it's noon nap now—
the boy wakes; sits up in his bed
and then his mother tells him about me,
of cannibal old me; how I'm abroad
upon the deep, but will come back
to dance him once again.
  STARBUCK.
Mary,
my own Mary promised that my boy
each morning should be carried
to the hill to catch the first glimpse
of his father's sail! Yes, yes,
no more! We head back for Nantucket!
Come, Captain, study the course
and let's away! See-see! The boy's face
from the window! The boy's hand on the hill.

(AHAB *makes no reply. A long pause.*)

  AHAB. (*Wondering to himself.*)
What inscrutable, unearthly thing
commands me? Is Ahab—Ahab?
Is it I or God that lifts this arm?
If the great sun move not of himself
but is an errand boy in heaven;
how then does this brain think thoughts
unless God does that thinking?
By heaven, man—we're turned around this world
like yonder windlass, Fate's the handspike;
and all the time—that smiling sky
and this unsounded sea!
Aye, it's a mild, mild wind

And a mild-looking sky. The air
smells now as if it blew from meadows far away. . . .
They have been making hay somewhere
under the slopes of the Andes, Starbuck,
and the mowers now are sleeping in the new-mown
    hay. . . .

(*A silence. Then suddenly.*)

MASTHEAD.
There she blows!
  AHAB.
Where?
  MASTHEAD.
Leeward, sir.
  AHAB.
A hump like a snow hill!
O, ye sweet powers of air!—It's *Moby Dick!*

(*MUSIC: A very low tympani roll, more a disturbance
    of the air than an outright sound. The excited voices
    of the crew grow louder as the* SAILORS *crowd on to
    the Forestage.*)

MASTHEAD.
There she blows! There! *There!* she blows,
she blows!
  AHAB.
Where away?
  MASTHEAD.
On the lee-beam, sir—two miles off!
  TASHTEGO.
There go flukes!

(VOICES *and MUSIC louder.*)

AHAB.
T'gallant sails—stunsails! Alow, aloft.
And on both sides! She blows!
She blows! She blows! God! What a spout!

STARBUCK.
The same! The same great silent spout
we've seen by moonlight—!
STUBB.
He's heading straight to leeward, sir,
and dead away from us.
FLASK.
He can't have seen the ship, sir.
AHAB.
Hard down at the helm! *Now—Moby Dick!*
I clutch thy heart at last!

(*LIGHTS change. MUSIC and EFFECTS louder.*)

STARBUCK.
Lower the boats!
MASTHEAD.
There she blows!—she blows!—she blows!

(*His cries are echoed in excited chorus by the* CREW.
*Frenzied movement as the "whale-boat" is pushed
out into the SPOTLIGHT Forestage and the* MEN
clamber to their places at the "oars.")

STUBB.
Blow on, and split your spout, old whale,
the crazy fiend himself is after ye!
Blow! Blow! Blister yer lungs—
Ahab'll dam off yer blood.
ISHMAEL.
Aye, Stubb, ye speak for all of us!
We are but one man, not thirty—
This man's valour, that man's fear—
and guilt and guiltiness—all welded
into oneness—all directed to that fatal goal
which Ahab, our one lord and keel, is pointing to—
all striving to seek out the thing that might destroy us!
STUBB.
Oars!!

(ALL *join in the violent rhythmic gestures of rowing.*)

ISHMAEL. (*Whispering.*)
Like noiseless nautilus shells, our prows
race forward toward the unsuspecting prey.
   FLASK. (*In a sort of whispered shout.*)
Oars! Oars! Grip yer oars, and clutch yer souls, now!
God, men—*pull!*
   STUBB.
Who is it dropped an anchor overboard?
We don't budge an inch! Don't hurry, boys!
Take plenty o' time—but *somebody*—please—
please burst a blood vessel, will ye?
   FLASK.
Roar and pull my thunder-bolts!
   STUBB. (*Suddenly shouting.*)
Sing out and *say* something!
(*There begins now the hoarse, steady, quick-paced chant-
ing of "Pull!—Pull!"*)
Pull, babes—pull, sucklings! Pull!
What are ye *hurrying* for?
Softly, steadily, just pull!
And keep pulling!—that's all, just crack
your backbones! Bite yer knives in two—that's all!
And take it *easy*—why not take it *easy*—
and burst your livers and your lungs!
   STARBUCK.
There she blows!

(*MUSIC EFFECT.*)

   FLASK.
                  Christ!—see the suds he makes
and what a hump!

(CHORUS *continues louder and quicker, "Pull!—Pull!"*)

   STUBB.
I tell ye what it is, men—

it's against my religion to get mad!
But, pull, pull, pull, *pull!*
What d'ye say, Tashtego? Tash-
are you the man to snap yer spine in two
and twenty pieces for the honour of the "Pequod"?
What d'ye say?
  TASHTEGO.
I say pull like goddam—!

  (*The other savage harpooners,* DAGGOO *and* QUEEQUEB,
    join TASHTEGO *in wild war-whoops which blend with
    the mounting chorus of "Pull!—Pull!" Suddenly*
    AHAB *moves forward between the rowing sailors, into
    the light. He raises his hand and at this signal all
    movement and sound is instantly cut off. Silence.*
    ALL *stare with fascinated wondering eyes at the
    "whale" before them.*)

  AHAB. (*Very quietly.*)
Harpoons . . .
  ISHMAEL.
Our three tigers, Queequeg, Tashtego and Daggoo
together point their barbs.
  STUBB. (*In a hoarse whisper.*)
Give him the long, stroke, stroke, Tashtego!
Start him, Tash, my boy!—but cool!—keep cool!
Cucumbers is the word, boy—easy—
(*Still whispering but with a sudden burst of vehemence.*)
Just raise the buried dead perpendicular
out of their graves, that's all!
  ISHMAEL.
The ocean's grown more calm—seems a noon meadow—
  AHAB. (*In a whisper.*)
Now—!
  ISHMAEL.
A gentle joyousness, a mighty mildness
of repose in swiftness invests
the grazing whale.
  AHAB. (*Still whispering.*)
            —Harpoons!

ISHMAEL.
Projecting from the creature's back
like to some flag-staff, there's a shattered lance
where sea-fowl perch and rock
streaming their tail-feathers like pennons—

(*Silence. Then* AHAB *bows his head, and howling their
three war-whoops, the* SAVAGES *fling out harpoons.*)

TASHTEGO.
Woo-hooooo!
DAGGOO.
Kee-heee!
QUEEQUEG.
Kaa-la-loo!

(*A swift LIGHT change. A hurrying rumble of big
DRUMS and a roar of noise like the rushing of
WIND.*)

STUBB.
There go flukes!
TASHTEGO.
Him fast! *Him fast!*
STARBUCK.
Line—*line!*

(*SOUND EFFECTS: Louder.*)

ISHMAEL.
The headlong rushing monster yanks us forward
towards the sun! Our boat leaves such a furrow
as when a cannon-ball, missent, becomes a plough-share
and turns up the level field!
STUBB.
By salt and hemp, but this swift motion, boys—
creeps up the legs, eh?—tingles, tingles at the heart!
ISHMAEL.
The humming line is tighter than a harp-string.

STARBUCK.
You'd think we're riding on two keels,
one cleaving water and the other air—

ISHMAEL.
The vibrating, cracking craft cants over
her spasmodic, gunwhales into the sea—
and on we rush—!

STUBB.
                 He's going to sound!

ISHMAEL.
He yaws and falters in his flight
and sideways rolls up towards the sky
one beating fin. So have I seen a bird
with clipped wing, making affrighted
broken circles in the air. The bird has voice
though, and the fear of this dumb brute is chained up
and enchanted in him. The sight is pitiful.
Yet his amazing hulk and jaw and tail's
enough to appall the stoutest man who pities. . . .

STUBB.
Look out, boys—there he goes—!

ISHMAEL.
Warningly he waves his bannered flukes in air—
the marble body arches high—the great god
reveals himself—! Then sounds—

(*All NOISE and EFFECTS abruptly fade into silence. A
    pause.*)

AHAB.

He'll breach— Aye, in an hour he'll breach. . . .

ISHMAEL.
Dipping on the wing
over the agitated pool he leaves
the sea birds linger longingly . . .

AHAB.
                   an hour . . .

ISHMAEL.
Oars apeak and paddles down,
Our three boats stilly float
awaiting Moby Dick's return. . . .

No groan or cry; no ripple, not a bubble . . .

What landsmen could believe
that under all that silence
the utmost monster of the deep
is writhing, wrenching in its agony;
the great Leviathan, by this thin thread,
suspended like the big weight of an eight-day clock?

STUBB. (*Ironically.*) We'll hear more from Leviathan; he'll strike the hour. . . .

(*A low nervous laugh at this from some of the* MEN; *it is quickly cut off. Silence again.*)

STARBUCK. (*Half to himself.*) Leviathan . . . "Can'st thou fill his skin with irons? Or his head with fish-spears?—"

STUBB. (*Irritably.*) Quote us no scriptures, Mrs. Starbuck, d'ye mind?

STARBUCK. (*Raising his voice slightly.*) "The sword of him that layeth at him cannot hold, he esteemeth iron as straw; darts are as stubble; he laugheth at the shaking of a spear!"

AHAB. He stirs!

(*MUSIC and SOUND EFFECTS.*)

STUBB.
Haul in—Haul in! He's rising!
That's you, Mr. Starbuck; Ye've called him up to pray for us.

(*More laughter—excited laughter—as the* MEN *struggle to haul in the line.*)

ISHMAEL.
Our line vibrates in the water—
conducting up to us, as by magnetic wires,
the life and death throbs of the whale—

Peering down we now, profoundly see
a white and living spot with wonderful celerity
uprising, magnifying as it rises. . . .

SAILORS.
She breaches . . . breaches . . .

ISHMAEL.
       The waters, in broad circles
slowly swell around us; now suddenly upheaves
as sideways sliding from a submerged berg of ice,
A rumbling is heard; a subterraneous hum. . . .

(EFFECTS.)

AHAB.
Breach your last to the sun, old Moby Dick!
Thy hour and thy harpoon are at hand!

ISHMAEL.
A glittering mouth yawns under us
an open marble tomb—

VOICES.
       The Jaw!—The Jaw!

ISHMAEL.
Slowly, feelingly, in the manner of a biting shark,
he takes our bows full in his mouth
shaking the slight cedar as a mildly cruel cat
her mouse. Gunwhales bend, collapse and snap,
both jaws, enormous shears,
bite our frail craft in twain!

*(As the EFFECTS grow to a crescendo, the LIGHTS
BLACK OUT. Only* ISHMAEL *is still seen. But presently
there is an indication of the scattered* CREW *clambering
aboard the "Pequod.")*

The attentive ship comes bearing to our rescue,
picks up floating mariners, tubs, oars,

and broken lances—whatever can be caught at.

With blood-shot blinded eyes,
the white brine caking in his wrinkles,
Ahab is helped up to the deck. . . .
   FLASK. (*Under his breath to* STUBB.)
His ivory leg, it's snapped—
   STUBB.
Aye, nothing's left there
But a short sharp splinter—it's an omen, Flask—and
    bad—
   AHAB.
The harpoon . . . the harpoon, is it safe?
   STUBB. (*As though speaking to a sick man.*)
Aye, sir. . . . Here.
   AHAB.
Help me up, men. . . . Let me stand. . . . So. . . . So.
(*Shouting up to the* MASTHEAD.)
Aloft there! What d'ye see?
   MASTHEAD.
Nothing, Cap'n.
   AHAB.
I've oversailed him! How! Got the start!
Aye, he's chasing *me*, and not I him.
Are any missing?
   STUBB.
No, sir. Just little Pip, sir.
   STARBUCK.
A bad beginning, sir.
   STUBB.
Aye, an omen, a bad omen. . . .
   AHAB.
Omen? Omen? If the gods would speak to man
they'll speak outright; not shake their heads
and give an old wives' darkling hint. Hands off!
You two are of mankind; old Ahab stands alone
among the millions of the peopled earth,
nor gods nor men his neighbours! How now . . .

(*Silence.*)
Aloft there! What d'ye see?
   MASTHEAD.
Nothing, sir. 'Tis growing very dark. . . .
   AHAB.
Brace sharper! Crowd her into the wind's eye.
Give me something for a cane. That shivered lance will do.
   STARBUCK.
Great God! But for one single instant show thyself,
Never, never wilt thou capture him, old man!

In Jesus' name, no more of this!
Twice stove to splinters; thy very leg
again snatched out from under thee,
and all good angels mobbing thee
with warnings; what more would'st thou have?
Shall we keep chasing him until he swamps
the last of us? Shall we be towed by him
to the eternal world?
   AHAB.
Starbuck—of late I'm strangely moved
to thee; aye, ever since we both saw—
thou know'st what—in one another's eyes.
But in this matter of the whale; Starbuck,
be thy face's front to me as in the palm
of this my hand—a lipless and unfeatured
blank. Ahab is forever Ahab, man!
I am the fate's lieutenant; under orders.
Ye see an old man cut down to the stump,
leaning on a shivered lance; propped
on a lonely foot; 'tis Ahab . . . Ahab's
body's part. But Ahab's soul's a centipede
that moves upon a hundred legs. You see
me strained, half-stranded as ropes that tow
dismasted frigates in a gale. But ere I'll break,
ye'll hear me crack! Till ye hear *that*,—
know Ahab's hawser tows his purpose yet!
   MASTHEAD.
There she blows—

AHAB.

There! There! To leeward still that leaping spout!
The eternal sap runs in old Ahab's bones again!

MASTHEAD.

She blows! . . . She blows!

AHAB.

Dead to leeward . . .
He travels faster than I thought for . . .
(*Then briskly.*)
Lower the spare boats! Lower all!
Mr. Starbuck, stay on board and keep the ship.
Hold clear of us, but near us—

STUBB.

Flukes! Look there, he's come about!
The old white demon's changed his course!

MASTHEAD.

She blows! . . .

AHAB.

About—about!
Come down, all but the look-outs!
Man the braces!

STARBUCK. (*To himself.*)

Against the wind he steers now for the open jaw.
I disobey my God, obeying him!

AHAB.

Aloft there! Keep him nailed!

MASTHEAD.

Aye, sir!

AHAB.

All hands to the rigging of the boats!
Mastheaders—sing out for every spout!
Aye, though he spout ten times a second!
Harpooneers,—the irons—I'll ten times
girdle the unmeasured globe, and dive
straight through it, but I'll slay him yet!
Starbuck . . . .

STARBUCK.

        Sir?

AHAB.

Some ships sail from their ports,
and ever afterwards are missing, Starbuck.

STARBUCK.

Truth, sir, saddest truth!

AHAB.

Some men die at ebb tide, some at low water,
some at the full of the blood;—and I feel now
much like a billow that's one crested comb, Starbuck.
I am old. Shake hands with me.

STARBUCK.

Oh, captain—My Captain!—noble heart, go not!

AHAB.

Lower away! Stand by the crew!

FLASK.

The sharks! Look, how they come!—

VOICES OF THE CREW.

The sharks—!

(Hesitant and fearful, the MEN *move to their places and resume their oars.)*

STARBUCK.

Heart of wrought steel!—lowering thy keel
among the ravening sharks!

AHAB.

Oars!

(The rowing starts again. This time the mood is grim, the MEN *bending and pulling rapidly but in silence, except for their gasping breaths.)*

ISHMAEL.

The sharks are biting at our plying oars;
the blades are jagg'd and crushed, and leave
small splinters in the sea at every dip.

AHAB.

Those teeth'll give new rowlocks to your oars!
Pull on—!

FLASK.
            But every bite, sir,
and the blades grow smaller!
    AHAB.
They'll last long enough.—Pull on!
    STUBB.
He's sounding, but he'll breach now, quick!
    ISHMAEL.
The boats dart forward to attack,
as all bedraggled with the trailing lines—
maddened by fresh irons corroding in him—
the white whale breaches—

                (MUSIC, EFFECTS.)

    AHAB.
Beach me!—Beach me there—on that white back—
    ISHMAEL.
The whale has turned—he meets our charge—
    AHAB.
Forehead to forehead, Moby Dick!
    ISHMAEL.
With open jaws and lashing tail,
all heedless of our darting lances,
on every side he crosses and recrosses,
tangling the lines so that they warp our boats
each minute to the planted irons in him—
    AHAB. (*In a terrible whisper.*)
O, ye sweet powers of air—now hug me close!
    ISHMAEL.
Caught—twisted—corkscrewed
in the mazes of the line, the loose harpoons
and lances with their bristling barbs
come flashing, dripping, to the bows of Ahab's boat—
    AHAB.
I grin at thee, thou grinning whale!
The lance. I want his heart. . . .

*(The LIGHTS DIM. MUSIC, or rather, a sickly pulsing
    sort of sound, grows louder, louder.)*

ISHMAEL. (*Hushed, horrified.*)
He slowly churns with his sharp lance
into the fish . . . and keeps it there . . .
and churns . . . and churns . . .

AHAB.
I'm growing blind; I may not grope my way; is't night?

ISHMAEL.
—and churns . . . and churns. . . .
As though he sought to feel after some gold watch
the whale had swallowed; and feared
to break it, ere he could hook it out. . . .

AHAB.
His heart . . . I'll have his heart. . . .

ISHMAEL.
Gush after gush of clotted gore
shoot up into the frightened air!

AHAB.
His heart!

(*MUSIC louder.*)

ISHMAEL.
Starting from its dying trance;
sensing the shadow of the nearing ship;—
it may be, too—acknowledging the Pequod
as a nobler foe—the white, humped monster
whirls and bears down on its black advancing prow!

SAILORS.
The whale! The ship!

ISHMAEL.
Still the black prow advances, and the whale attacks!
The smitten bow-ends of the two blanks burst through!

(*SOUND EFFECTS.*)

SAILORS.
The ship! The ship!

ISHMAEL.
The mighty buttress of that forehead
smites the starboard bow!

Again—and once again!
(*Wild cries.*)
                              till men and timbers reel!
And through the breach we hear the waters pour!
    AHAB.
Is this the end of all my bursting prayers?
All my life-long fidelities? Nay-nay— Up helm!

(*The LIGHTS DIM further. MUSIC and EFFECTS.*)

    STUBB.
The ship! Great God, where is the ship?
    ISHMAEL.
Only the topmost spars stand clear,—
Once lofty perches, where the harpooners—
fixed by infatuation or fidelity or fate—
maintain their sinking look-outs on the sea.
    AHAB.
Thou uncracked keel; god-bullied hull,
must ye then perish, and without me?
Give me the last harpoon!
(*Only* AHAB *is in light.*)
Now, Moby Dick—!
Thou all destroying but unconquering!
For hate's sake I spit my breath at thee!
From hell's heart I stab at thee—!

(*As he throws out the harpoon the LIGHT vanishes. A
     faint GLOW appears on* ISHMAEL.)

    ISHMAEL.
The harpoon darts—darts true!
The stricken whale flies forward!
The harpoon line smokes through the grooves—
runs foul—and Ahab stoops to clear it.
But the flying turn has caught him
round the neck; and voicelessly—
as Turkish mutes bow-string their victims—
Ahab is gone!

The white whale dies. . . .
Shrouded in a drooping veil of mist, it hovers
for a moment in the rainbowed air;
falls swamping back into the deep, and then—head-on—
comes churning his great tail among our boats!
Dashing them together like two rolling husks
on a surf-beaten beach. Moby Dick
bears Ahab's fatal iron down with him,
down into a boiling maelstrom where the wrecks,—
all bits and flakes of odorous cedar,—
whirl round and round like nutmeg
in a bowl of punch that's swiftly stirred.
The greedy vortex seizes on the ship, its crew,
each floating oar, and every lance-pole—
carries the last, small chip of the Pequod out of sight . . .
(*A pause.* ISHMAEL *moves forward into another LIGHT
in the Center of the Stage.*)
. . . Out of the sight of Ishmael. . . .
For I, and only I, escaped to tell thee.

On the second day a ship drew near me.
It was the "Rachel" that in her search
after her missing children
only found another orphan.

(ISHMAEL *closes the prompt-book. After a moment some
of the other* ACTORS *move out of the darkness to
Center Stage, picking up their overcoats and putting
them on.* AHAB *goes to* THE STAGE MANAGER'S *table.
But he is* AHAB *no longer, and as he retrieves his
wide-brimmed hat and lights a cigar, he is, once more,
every inch*—THE GOVERNOR. *The* OTHERS *have
started out via the Stage door.* THE YOUNG ACTOR
rises and looks at the old actor-manager.)

THE GOVERNOR. You can take down the curtain.

(*He turns and walks away. After a moment:*)

THE CURTAIN FALLS

OTHER TITLES AVAILABLE FROM SAMUEL FRENCH

GLENGARRY GLEN ROSS
David Mamet

Comedic Drama / 7m / 2 Interiors

This scalding comedy took Broadway and London by storm and won the 1984 Pulitzer Prize. Here is Mamet at his very best, writing about small-time, cutthroat real estate salesmen trying to grind out a living by pushing plots of land on reluctant buyers in a never-ending scramble for their share of the American dream. Revived on Broadway in 2006 this masterpiece of American drama became a celebrated film which starred Al Pacino, Jack Lemmon, Alec Baldwin and Alan Arkin.

"Crackling tension... ferocious comedy and drama."
– New York Times

"Wonderfully funny... A play to see, remember and cherish."
– New York Post